YOU NEVER KNOW
A Legend of
the Lamed-vavniks

BY Francine Prose
PICTURES BY Mark Podwal

Greenwillow Books, New York

Gouache and colored pencils were used for the full-color art.
The text type is Seagull Light.
Text copyright © 1998 by Francine Prose
Illustrations copyright © 1998 by Mark Podwal
All rights reserved. No part of this book may be reproduced or
utilized in any form or by any means, electronic or mechanical,
including photocopying, recording, or by any information
system, without permission in writing from the Publisher,
Greenwillow Books, a division of William Morrow & Company, Inc.,
1350 Avenue of the Americas, New York, NY 10019.
Printed in Hong Kong by South China Printing Company (1988) Ltd.
http://www.williammorrow.com
First Edition   10   9   8   7   6   5   4   3   2   1

Library of Congress Cataloging-in-Publication Data
Prose, Francine, (date)
You never know: a legend of the Lamed-vavniks /
by Francine Prose ; pictures by Mark Podwal.
p.   cm.
Summary: Though mocked by the rest of the villagers, poor
Schmuel the shoemaker turns out to be a very special person.
ISBN 0-688-15806-4 (trade).   ISBN 0-688-15807-2 (lib. bdg.)
[1. Jews—Folklore.   2. Folklore.]
I. Podwal, Mark H., (date) ill.   II. Title.
PZ8.1.P9348Yo   1998   398.2'089924—dc21
97-24764   CIP   AC

For Bruno and Leon
—F. P.

For my mother
—M. P.

or forty days and forty nights no rain fell on the town of Plotchnik.

Every green thing turned brown, and a dry wind rattled the branches. The thirsty cows stopped giving milk. Fish circled the shallow muddy puddle that was once a deep cold lake.

In the synagogue the Rabbi prayed, "Lord of the universe, favor us with rain."

Not a drop of rain fell.

The rich man prayed the same prayer. Not a trickle.

The teacher, the doctor, the lawyer, the butcher, the baker, the candlestick maker prayed.

Not one wispy cloud appeared in the clear blue sky.

"Maybe I should pray," came a meek voice from the back
of the synagogue.

It was Schmuel the Shoemaker. Poor Schmuel, they called
him. Poor Stupid Schmuel, they called him secretly, because
he often forgot to charge his customers for fixing their shoes,
and if you forgot to pay Schmuel, Schmuel forgot to ask.

When a beggar came through town, Schmuel gave him
free shoes.

Once, when a fierce bear appeared in the streets and
everyone hid in their houses, Stupid Schmuel gave the
bear water—and the bear went back to the woods.

Whenever there was trouble, somehow Schmuel was—
magically!—always right there, ready to help, smiling
and singing to himself.

No one cared if Poor Schmuel prayed. If God ignored
the town elders, why would He listen to Schmuel—
who couldn't even read the prayers?

"Please, God, send rain," prayed Poor Schmuel.

Thunder grumbled in the distance. The sky turned black as coal. Raindrops tapped the roofs, and people ran out with their heads tilted back, catching the drops in their mouths.

"We prayed for rain, and God listened!" said the Rabbi, the rich man, the teacher, the doctor, the lawyer, the butcher, the baker, and the candlestick maker.

Poor Schmuel said nothing. Smiling and singing to himself, he went home to his tumbledown cobbler shop.

It rained for forty days and nights. Soon the cows and fish were swimming through the streets. Water climbed all the way up to the steps of the synagogue—where now the people of Plotchnik prayed for the rain to stop.

"Lord of the universe," prayed the Rabbi. "Take back your generous gifts."

The wind howled, and the rain drove sideways against the windows.

The rich man, the lawyer, the doctor, the teacher, the butcher, the baker, and the candlestick maker prayed with the Rabbi.

Lightning crackled in the sky, and a cold wind blew out the lamps and the candles.

In the dark they heard Schmuel pray, "God, please make it stop raining."

All at once the rain stopped. The sun came out.

But now no one left the synagogue. They just stood there, blinking, staring at Schmuel. And Schmuel, smiling and singing to himself, went home to his tumbledown cobbler shop.

After he was gone, people said, "Why does God listen to Poor Schmuel and not to us?"

"I will think about it," said the Rabbi.

That night the Rabbi had a dream.
He dreamed of menorahs
with thirty-six candles.

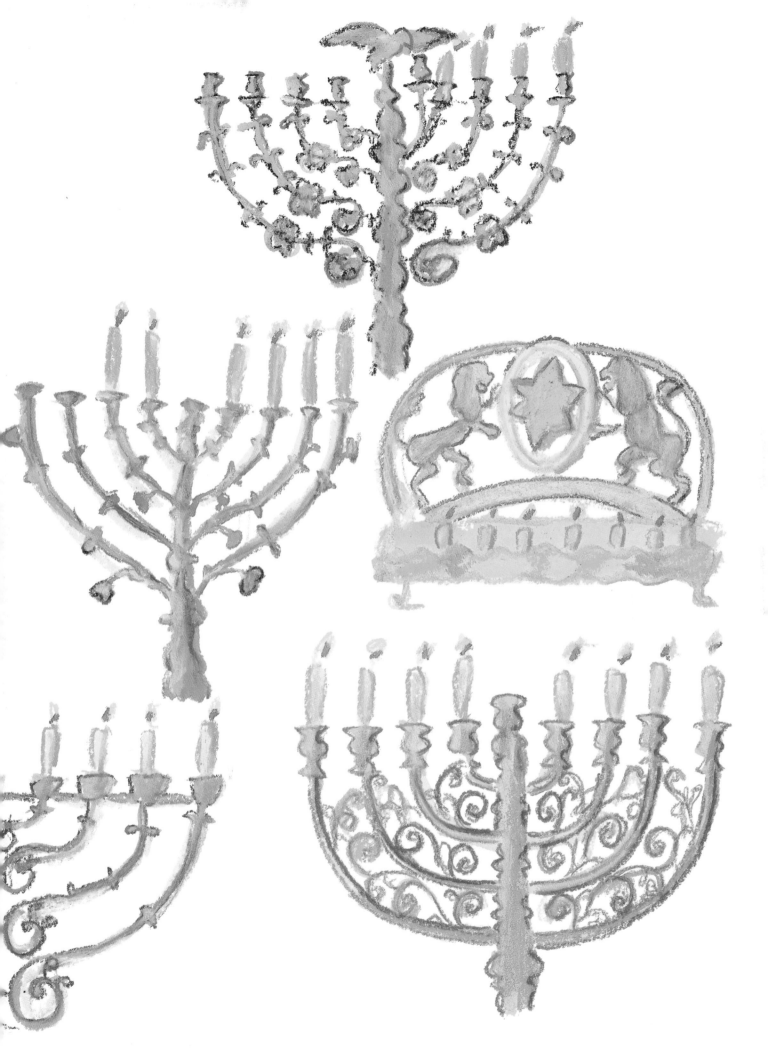

He dreamed he saw a door in the sky, bordered
by thirty-six stars, and when he walked through
the door, he saw a magnificent feast.
Thirty-six men sat at a banquet table, all of them
dressed in white, their faces radiant with light.
And who was sitting near the head of the table?
Poor Schmuel!

Suddenly the Rabbi understood why Schmuel's prayers had made the rain stop. And now he knew that Schmuel had made the rain start, as well.

In the morning the Rabbi rushed to the synagogue and called the people together.

"Listen!" he cried. "Our own Poor Schmuel is one of the holy Lamed-vavniks!"

"The what?" asked the butcher.

"The thirty-six righteous people," said the Rabbi.

"How many?" asked the baker.

"Thirty-six," said the Rabbi.

"The thirty-six who?" asked the candlestick maker.

"Lamed-vavniks," repeated the Rabbi.

The Rabbi continued. "An ancient legend tells us that scattered throughout the world there live thirty-six of these holy people. No one knows who they are. Many of them are humble, poor, ragged, homeless wanderers. And yet these people are so good, so kind, so just and righteous, they have God's ear. The world could not get along without them, so much depends on their prayers. Even the weather in Plotchnik."

"And our Schmuel is one of the thirty-six!" cried the butcher.

"What good fortune that he should be living here in Plotchnik!" said the baker.

"Let's go find him and tell the world that he lives here," said the candlestick maker.

"Plotchnik will become famous!" announced the rich man. "Travelers will come to see him. Maybe our town will make money!"

The townspeople rushed to the cobbler shop. There they found Schmuel's tools and the shoes that he'd fixed and polished and left without charging their owners. But Schmuel was gone.

If you are one of the thirty-six Lamed-vavniks, it must remain a secret. If anyone discovers who you really are, you will lose your special powers. That is part of being a Lamed-vavnik.

No one in Plotchnik ever found out where Poor Schmuel went.

Someone saw him in Vilna, digging ditches.

Someone spotted him begging outside the gates of Jerusalem.

Someone saw him in New York, where he had a little junk shop.

And someone saw him in your town, fixing your shoes and forgetting to charge you.

A few months after Schmuel left, a new cobbler
came to Plotchnik.

His name was Yakov, and he was poor, but no
one called him Poor Stupid Yakov. Everyone
was kind to him.

After all, you never know.

AUTHOR'S NOTE

You Never Know is based on the ancient legend of the Lamed-vavniks. According to Jewish tradition, there are at every moment, in every generation, thirty-six (Lamed-vav means "thirty-six" in Hebrew) righteous individuals living in secret throughout the world. They never make their presence known unless there is some threat to the community—and after the danger is over, they disappear back into obscurity. If the generation is worthy, one of these thirty-six hidden saints will become the Messiah.

According to André Schwartz-Bart, whose celebrated novel The Last of the Just was inspired by this legend, these unknown, humble people are so beloved of God that whenever one of them rises into heaven, God sets forward the clock of the Last Judgment by one minute. "The Lamed-Vov are the hearts of the world multiplied, and into them, as into one receptacle, pour all our griefs."

Added up, the number of candles we light in the menorah during Hanukkah totals thirty-six—a reminder meant to rekindle our faith in the Lamed-vavniks.

Bibliography:

Ausubel, Nathan. A Treasury of Jewish Folklore. New York: Crown, 1958.

Scholem, Gershom. The Messianic Idea in Judaism.
New York: Schocken Books, 1971.

Schwartz-Bart, André. The Last of the Just. New York: Atheneum, 1960.

J

398   Prose, Francine.
P   You never know.